WHEN WILLIAM LOST A FRIEND

T STEELE PETRY

Copyright © 2023 T STEELE PETRY.

All rights reserved. No part of this book may be reproduced, stored, or transmitted by any means—whether auditory, graphic, mechanical, or electronic—without written permission of both publisher and author, except in the case of brief excerpts used in critical articles and reviews. Unauthorized reproduction of any part of this work is illegal and is punishable by law.

ISBN: 979-8-89031-483-3 (sc)
ISBN: 979-8-89031-484-0 (hc)
ISBN: 979-8-89031-485-7 (e)

Because of the dynamic nature of the Internet, any web addresses or links contained in this book may have changed since publication and may no longer be valid. The views expressed in this work are solely those of the author and do not necessarily reflect the views of the publisher, and the publisher hereby disclaims any responsibility for them.

One Galleria Blvd., Suite 1900, Metairie, LA 70001
(504) 702-6708
1-888-421-2397

BEST FRIENDS FOREVER

William and Trevor were the best of friends
for most of their 18 years.

Life was terrific most of the time,
but the future would bring many tears.

The boys had grown up together,
and they were essentially family.

William saw Trevor every day of the week,
but the signs he was not able to see.

Football, wrestling, and track were sports,
that both of the boys had played.

They knew all of their teammates,
and many friends were also made.

William and Trevor
were often together
the entire weekend long.

They loved to play,
for many hours a day,
table top tennis, (aka ping pong).

They had been playing ping pong for years,
and both were getting good.

Each had brand new paddles
that weren't just made of wood.

The boys were always together,
essentially every day.

And when one was asked a question,
each knew what the other would say.

They had spent the night out camping
a countless number of times.

They saw each other as brothers,
but Will still missed the signs.

TROUBLE IS BREWING

William and Trevor were rarely apart,
the best that I recall.

They swam in the lake that summer,
and they went hunting in the fall.

Winter was the next season to arrive,
and that's when Will's world
came tumbling
down.

He first started to notice,
and soon he wondered,
why Trevor was wearing a frown.

Trevor had always proclaimed his love
with a girl from across the bay,

Announcing he would love Maggie forever,
or until cold in the casket he lay.

Maggie and Trevor
used to speak for hours together,
multiple times a day.

But now they would go,
many days in a row,
with nothing at all to say.

"Even though I tried,
The spark seems to have died,"
said Trevor as he cried,
slowly wiping the salty tears away.

GIRLS ENTER THE SCENE

Will remembered back before
girls ever even entered the scene.

Most of the girls he knew were nice,
but a few were very mean.

He could never really understand
how any person could be so cruel.

Watching and laughing as a normal boy
acted like a total fool.

Trevor dated Maggie for over a year,
and they were as happy as they could be.

Every decision Trevor made that year
always started with 'we'.

William and Trevor would still get together
to play a little pong.

They shared many hours of fun and laughs,
and time would sail along.

In the beautiful weather,
they went hunting together,
in the autumn of that year.

With William still having no clue at all,
that the end was very near.

THE SIGNS

It was right before the holiday season,
when Maggie and Trevor finally broke up.

Around the same time
that William adopted
a new English Setter pup.

The new pup required much of William's time,
to train him how to hunt.

Some days the puppy learned quickly,
other days it was time to punt.

The perky puppy performed pretty well over all,
patience and persistence provided the perfect key.

So the puppy pretty well kept Will pretty busy,
and the signs he was not able to see.

He would still call Trevor twice every day,
and he also left many voice mails for him.

Will sent multiple text messages to Trevor,
wondering if he wanted to work out at the gym.

He figured Trevor must be staying very busy,
for they hardly spoke at all.

When Trevor was actually
home alone in his room,
staring at an empty wall.

THE CAR

Trevor had recently turned eighteen,
and his dad bought him a cool used car.

He drove himself to school and work,
for to walk was way too far.

Trevor really loved that car,
and he always kept it clean.

The tan interior was simply spotless,
and its color was forest green.

It became Trevor's pride and joy,
and he was proud to drive it around.

If Trevor was not at school or work,
in that car he could be found.

It was a classic older car;
a muscle car from way back when,
with
a
cool
white stripe
right down the middle,
from the grill to the spoiler end.

William and Trevor had fun in that car,
as they traveled from here to there.
I will tell you
a true tale I recall,
that involves a grizzly bear.

The two boys had hiked many a mile…… in weather quite vile,
and had finally arrived…….. tired but alive,
when the big grizzly came around the bend.
They were standing too near,
so they dropped all their gear,
and ran with great fear,
knowing that the bear was not their friend.

They jumped in the car,
which with luck was not far,
and proceeded to lock every door.
I guess they thought that the bear
was somehow aware,
what the handle to the door was for.

I still laugh till I cry,
I tell you no lie,
whenever I relate this tale.

And it is so true,
this tale I'm telling you,
just like Moby was a big white whale.

That old car would soon play,
a huge role every day,
and change everyone's lives forever.

It would cause Will to meet,
his soulmate so sweet,
and they would spend forever together.

The length of their meeting
was perhaps very fleeting,
but they both felt it right away

Fate brought them together
despite the cold weather,
because of a fateful day.

THE FATEFUL DAY

Trevor rarely returned Will's texts or calls,
and Will began to wonder why.

He was not at all prepared
to have said his last goodbye.

Will decided to stop by one day,
when Trevor was to be at home.

No one came when he pressed the bell,
and no one answered his phone.

William peered through
the dirty garage window,
when he heard a familiar sound.

The old car's engine was running strong,
but the door was still way down.

Will banged hard on the side entry door,
after he discovered the door was locked.

No answer was heard, or seen from within,
and entry through this door was blocked.

William had little time to decide
how to best get inside
through the large garage door

He punched in several numbers
and to his great wonder
his birthday was indeed the correct four

As the
big door started rising,
hoping Trevor was still surviving,
and that this day was just a horrible dream.

William felt so much rage,
like a lion in a cage,
and he very much wanted to scream.

When the garage door fully lifted,
William still stood tight fisted
as the thick toxic fumes billowed out.

And once the fumes had grown thin,
and William could see once again
he couldn't help but cry out and shout.

William ran to the old car where he found Trevor,
sitting there all alone.

Laying on the seat right next to him,
was Maggie's picture on his phone.

William tried hard to revive him,
after he first dialed nine one one.

But despite everyone's best attempt,
Trevor was actually gone.

THE FUNERAL

The funeral
was held
five days later,
a terribly sad affair!

Trevor was dressed in a fancy suit and tie,
something he never even liked to wear.

The lines were long
as his friends lined up
to pay their last respects.

Many had wondered
if something was wrong,
and now they had regrets.

Others agreed,
and said they believed,
that something had not felt right.

Old friends were now feeling guilty,
and many a tear
was shed that night.

Too bad Trevor,
must have never,
thought about forever;
and
This tremendous heartache his suicide would cause;
for
perhaps if he knew,
and had thought it through,
he might have avoided Satan's powerful claws.

KATIE

William met Katie at the funeral,
and this meeting was meant to be.

Despite the sad occasion,
they would soon be known as 'we'.

William and Katie were soulmates!
and they both knew it right away.

They married several years later,
and remain deeply in love today.

They both suffer from
Post Traumatic Stress Disorder,
deep down in their soul,
but
they are happy
they found each other!
For they make each other whole.

THE AFTERMATH

William still has frequent nightmares,
re-living that terrible day.

The memory remains so vivid,
and it will never go away!

William stays sad and sheds many tears,
unable to forget what he saw.

He is still trying to deal with the pain,
and his emotions are often raw.

Trevor's parents are also distraught,
after losing their only son.

There will never be another like Trevor!
of us all there is only one!!

Many of the students who Trevor had known
also met with a counsellor from school.

they wanted to understand all about suicide,
and learn to follow *The Golden Rule.

*(do unto others as you would have others do unto you)

TOUGH YEARS

Teen age years can be tough
for just about everyone.

But those hard times will eventually end,
just like the setting sun.

Something we need to remember,
a message that I send -

**WHEN TIMES GET TOUGH,
WE DON'T NEED TO BREAK,
WE MUST SIMPLY LEARN TO BEND.**

Just go with the flow,
is a phrase we all know,
that is very commonly heard.

Even if all you can hear,
from ear to ear,
is many a discouraging word.

LIFE IS WORTH LIVING

Life can occasionally spin out of control,
and it can happen to you.

Sometimes you cannot help yourself,
when you feel lonely and blue.

Please tell someone
if you feel that way,
before it is too late.

Violence and self harm are never the answer,
and should never be anyone's fate.

Everyone will have to face hardship
some time in their life.

People may do things that hurt you,
and cut you like a knife.

But you have value as a person,
to your god and others, too.

Remembering this is important,
and will help to get you through.

Everyone's life is there for the living,
so enjoy it the best you can.

And always remember your Lord above,
who will remain your biggest fan.

PLEASE

IF YOU HAVE A PLAN TO HURT YOURSELF OR OTHERS

PLEASE TAKE A DEEP BREATH AND WAIT

CALL 988 OR THE SUICIDE LINE

BEFORE IT IS TOO LATE

1-800-273-8255

LIFE IS WORTH LIVING!!

The end

T Steele Petry is a retired Family Physician who dedicated his life to caring for people of all ages for over 35 years. He has combined his talents of painting and poetry, accompanied with a desire to entertain and inform, into THE LITTLE SERIES books.

The Series is directed at children from the age of 2 through 9 depending on the readers skill level but a primary purpose of the Series is to promote an excellent bonding experience for both the reader and the child. T Steele Petry is a firm believer in the benefits of reading to a child as much as possible.

He also believes in passive learning and incorporates that into most of his books. This passive learning starts with what to do if you get lost in **LITTLE SALLY ON SAFARI** and continues throughout the Series.

T Steele Petry was born in Denver and lived in many parts of the country while growing up, including Alabama, Delaware, New Jersey, northern Wisconsin and Indiana where he has resided for the past 30 years. He was active in the Boy Scouts and achieved the rank of Eagle with a Bronze Palm.

He learned to respect nature and other people through his many experiences throughout the years and hopes to share a little knowledge along with fun entertainment through his works in THE LITTLE SERIES.

Along with his love for the outdoors he is an avid dog lover and sportsman.

www.ingramcontent.com/pod-product-compliance
Lightning Source LLC
LaVergne TN
LVHW070529070526
838199LV00073B/6734